W9-DGY-303

My Angel Named Herman

My Angel Named Herman

ELMER L. TOWNS

Thomas Nelson, Inc.

Nashville

Published in Nashville, Tennessee, by Tommy Nelson™,
a division of Thomas Nelson, Inc.

Scripture quoted is from the King James Version of the Bible.

Written by Elmer L. Towns
Cover Illustration by William Maughan
Interior Illustrations and Cover Sketch by Tony Sansevero
Executive Editor: Laura Minchew
Managing Editor: Beverly Phillips

Library of Congress Cataloging-in-Publication Data

Towns, Elmer L.
    My angel named Herman / Elmer L. Towns ; illustrated by William
Maughan.
        p.   cm.
    Summary: A young boy learns about the stars and the universe and
all of God's creation from the kindly janitor at his elementary school
who turns out to be even more special than he had seemed.
    ISBN 0-8499-5839-3
    [1. God—Fiction. 2. Astronomy—Fiction. 3. Guardian angels—
Fiction. 4. Angels—Fiction.] I. Maughan, William, ill. II. Title.
    PZ7.T6497Mg   1998
    [Fic]—dc21
                                                                98-4896
                                                                CIP
                                                                AC

Printed in the United States of America

98 99 00 01 02 03 BVG 9 8 7 6 5 4 3 2 1

Be not forgetful to entertain strangers: for thereby some have entertained angels unawares.

—Hebrews 13:2 (KJV)

INTRODUCTION

Did you know that angels have been called stars?

In the last chapter of the Bible, the book of Revelation, the writer says, "The seven stars are the angels of the seven churches" (Revelation 1:20 KJV).

That doesn't mean that the stars you see in the sky are angels . . . not at all. The stars you see on a dark night are really burning suns. They are millions of light-years away.

Angels are like people who think and feel and carry out orders. They have heavenly bodies, and sometimes they look like people you know. Angels do what God wants them to do, and at least one watches over you.

Both angels and stars shine—maybe that's why angels are called stars.

Some people have seen angels. That's why the Bible says, "Be not forgetful to entertain strangers: for thereby some have entertained angels unawares" (Hebrews 13:2 KJV).

That means you don't always know when you're talking to an angel.

See you around,
Herman

CHAPTER 1

That's a Big Star

Mom was late picking me up from soccer practice. The cold January wind blew faded yellow leaves across the empty soccer field. All the other soccer players were gone, and the coach was locking up the equipment. I zipped my jacket all the way up to the neck to stay warm. I wondered where Mom was. She seemed so busy, and kind of far away since she and Dad got the divorce. She had to work very hard and didn't have much time to talk. When she did get home, she just looked so tired . . .

I tried not to bother her with my things, but I hoped she remembered to come soon. The streetlight flickered on in front of the church across from school. Looking up into a darkening sky, I saw a faint evening star.

"That star's called Venus." A voice coming out of the darkness startled me and I jumped.

"And over there is Mercury." Whipping around I saw a grandfatherly man in a blue and green jacket. I had seen him before working around my school.

"I didn't mean to scare you," he said, his reassuring voice calming me. "I was out for my evening exercise when I saw you studying the stars." Then he stuck out a large, wrinkled hand.

I shook it and said, "My name is Jacob. I've seen you at school—you're the janitor, aren't you?"

"Well, I keep an eye on things. Make sure they are taken care of—I have a lot of work to do around here . . . my name's Herman, by the way."

His hand was rough from hard work, but it was a friendly hand. He said he had seen me around the halls.

"Do you *like* to clean things?" I asked. "I hate to clean my room. I wouldn't want to clean up all day long!"

"Oh, I like it all right." He chuckled. "I look at my work as a special assignment from God. He gives us all certain talents for doing certain things and puts us in just the right place at just the right time to do the most good.

"I like stars, too," Herman said. He must have read my mind, because that was just what I'd been thinking. I felt good talking about the stars. I liked any-one who liked stars.

3

"What's the name of that star?" I pointed to a brilliant light shining through the bare limbs of a tree.

"That's not a star." He laughed. "That's the Moon."

"What's the difference between a star and the Moon?" I asked, testing him.

"Well . . ." He shuffled his tennis shoes and sat down beside me on the bench.

"A star is a light, like a fire burning at night . . . or like a light in the refrigerator."

"Oh . . ." I thought about the bright stars that shone in my window. They weren't bright enough to read by.

"The Moon doesn't have any light of its own. The Moon is like a round mirror . . . it just reflects light from the Sun."

"Is Earth a star?" I asked.

"No . . . Earth does not shine like the Sun . . . Earth just reflects light," said Herman. He went on to explain that the

*"The Moon is like a round mirror . . .
it just reflects light from the Sun."*

Sun is a gigantic fire that can be seen millions of miles away. Also, because it is a fire, its rays are warm.

I almost wished for some of those warm rays at that moment. I was chilly and Mom was late. But suddenly I didn't mind waiting as much. My new friend could talk to me about the stars. I wanted to impress him, so I said:

"Our planet is the biggest and best . . ." I liked to think everything I owned was the biggest and the best.

"No . . ." My new friend shook his head slowly from side to side. "Jupiter is eleven times bigger than Earth. It's the biggest planet in our solar system."

"How do ya know?"

"Oh . . . I've been around."

"Errr . . ." I didn't know what to say about that. I hoped he didn't feel bad about being old or something. "Then Jupiter is the biggest thing in our solar system?" I asked.

"No . . . Jupiter is only a planet. The Sun is a burning star, and it is thousands of times bigger than Jupiter."

"How do ya know?"

"I've been around, remember?"

"So what's the biggest thing of all?" Talking to Herman was like eating potato chips. I wanted to know more about the stars and the solar system every time he told me something new.

"The Sun is so big . . . so *very* big . . . that if it were hollow, 1.3 million Earths could fit inside it."

"Wow . . . !" That sounded big, but I really didn't know how big a million was. "Is the Sun the biggest thing there is?"

"Oh, no . . . not at all," he said.

"What's bigger?"

"There's a star named Betelgeuse in the

Orion belt that, if it were hollow, could hold 90 million of our Suns."

"Wow . . ." My voice dropped in disbelief. I still didn't know how big a million was.

"And bigger than that . . . ," Herman continued, "there is, in the constellation of Hercules, a star that could hold 100 million stars like Betelgeuse." He stopped to see if I were listening. I was. I'd never known anyone who knew so much about stars and planets!

Herman went on. "The largest known star is Mu Cephi, which could hold 422 million stars the size of the one in Hercules."

"That's BIG!" was all I could say.

Herman's laugh told me that he knew I was impressed.

"Where did all these stars come from?" I asked, curious to know. If there were some little boys sitting in space, staring at my planet—like I was staring at theirs—I wanted to know where they came from.

"God made the stars." Herman formed his wrinkled hands into a circle as though he were making a snowball. "God's hands just shaped the stars, then He threw them into place."

"How do ya know?"

"Why, everybody knows He did it."

"Why did God make stars so big?"

"Because God is big . . . He's a big God," Herman said. "The universe is big . . . it has a lot of big stars . . . and big stars shine farther than little stars . . . big stars shine to the end of God's universe."

My curiosity was going 90 miles an hour. "How do ya know so much about stars?" I asked.

"All you have to do is look." He paused. "And you can see it all."

Then I saw the lights of Mom's station

wagon bouncing down the rough lane to the soccer field. I waved good-bye to my new friend as I ran to meet Mom. Because I liked stars, I decided that I liked Herman, too. Then turning, I yelled one last question, "Will you tell me more about stars later on?"

CHAPTER 2

Green Is God's Favorite Color

I stood motionless in front of a bulletin board in the school library. I loved pictures of faraway galaxies . . . dazzling red planets . . . amber and blue moons . . . dark purple comets . . . and gleaming yellow suns . . . all burning brightly on a black background.

I was wrapped up in the heavenly world before me. It was as if I had been lifted from Alan B. Shepherd School, and these objects were flashing by me at lightning speeds.

"Hello." A raspy voice startled me and interrupted my dreams. It was Herman.

"Didn't mean to make you jump," he added.

Herman wore the same blue and green jacket over his work clothes. He stopped sweeping and leaned on his push broom. He pulled a red bandanna from a rear pocket to wipe his hands. Then he leaned his broom against the wall and walked over beside me to look at the poster of the universe.

Pointing to a green planet, Herman asked, "Do you see what's different about Earth on this chart?" Like my grandfather, Herman always asked me something right before he told me something.

I studied the green circle.

"Earth is called a terrestrial planet," Herman said. He explained that Mercury, Venus, Earth, and Mars are closest to the

Sun. They all have hard, crusty surfaces. He pointed to Jupiter, Saturn, Uranus, Neptune, and Pluto, explaining that they are all gas giants, except Pluto, which is made up mostly of ice.

"Earth is green because it's the only planet that grows living things." Herman tucked his red bandanna back into his pocket. "None of the other planets grow things, so none of them are green."

Sure enough, none of the other heavenly bodies on the chart were green. Then I remembered something. When the astronauts took pictures of Earth, it was blue. They called it a blue marble . . . not a green marble. Herman must have been reading my thoughts. He explained, "Let me tell you why it's green. Certain gases from the photosynthesis process make green plants look blue." Then to make sure I understood, Herman said, "It's like the Blue Ridge Mountains of Virginia are green when you're up close, but they're blue from a distance."

How did Herman know that? I thought. Then I asked, "Are you sure you're not one of the teachers who's just helping sweep the floor?"

Herman chuckled.

"God made Earth in six days," he explained.

Then, looking out the window, Herman pointed to the sky. "God just said, 'I want Earth right here in the middle of space.' After He made it, He hurled Earth through space and it went speeding on its way."

"Just like that?" I asked.

Herman chuckled again.

"A lot of planets are just rocks . . . and dirt . . . and sand. But not Earth." He stopped to smile, as though he knew exactly how God did it. "God made water

"Earth is green because it's the only planet that grows living things."

and poured it into oceans, seas, and rivers . . . He separated the water from dry land.

"God made trees, grass, and flowers . . . and water made them grow to produce food to eat." Then Herman nodded his head. "God made animals, too, such as puppies and cows. God also made things grow in the waters—fish, shrimp, and crabs—the things you like to eat."

"How did God make all these things?" I asked curiously.

"God just spoke and then everything appeared."

"Oh."

"God made everything." Herman interrupted my thoughts by sweeping his hand for me to see everything in the schoolyard. Then his hand stopped abruptly when it pointed to some kids playing. "God made people, too."

"Why did God make people?" I asked.

"Because He likes them," Herman answered.

"Did God make aliens on other planets?" I asked, thinking about movies I'd seen. "Did God make E.T.?"

"What do you think . . . ?" He lowered his voice like he expected me to be disappointed. Then he asked another question on top of the question he had just asked.

"Can anything grow if there's no water . . . or trees . . . or grass?" He turned and pointed back to the bulletin board.

"See . . . only Earth is green." Herman smiled and waited for me to agree. "Only Earth grows food."

"Are you sure?"

"Positive!"

"Are you a retired astronaut?" I cautiously asked.

"No." Herman smiled. "But you can read about all these things in books or learn it from the Bible. God made all the planets. We don't know why God put people on this planet . . . He just did."

"Wow! What a great thought! But why'd God make Earth green?"

"Because . . . ," Herman said, winking at me, "green is God's favorite color."

CHAPTER 3

God Likes Stars

One night later that week, I was working on a science project with my new Christmas gift—a powerful telescope. The Moon would peek at me every once in a while from behind the dark thunderclouds. And even when it came out, I thought someone had turned down the dimmer, like when Mom dims the family room lights. The Moon was not as bright as it had been on other nights, and I could see only a few stars. I wondered why.

I'll ask Herman, I thought. *He knows everything about heaven.*

At school the next morning, I saw Herman pulling on the rope to raise the United States flag. I waved. "Good morning, Herman." It was early, and no one else was around.

He waved back with his big right hand, as he held the flag rope with the other. Then, as though he already knew what was on my mind, Herman asked, "Did you see those beautiful winter storm clouds move through last night?" Then he added, "That's called a front."

"Yeah . . ." I didn't know what else to say.

"There were some high cirrus clouds at 15,000 feet." Herman looked into the sky. "But they're gone . . . look, it's clear as glass this morning."

"I wanted to ask you something," I said as I stopped in front of Herman so that we were face-to-face. "I could only see a few stars last night . . . where do they hide?" I wondered to myself if they played hide-and-seek or something.

Herman laughed like he always did right before telling me something I wanted to know. "Stars don't hide. They stay right where God put them. Those high, thin clouds were racing much faster across heaven than those low-hanging thunder-clouds. When you were looking through those high clouds, it was like looking at the Sun through sunglasses."

Herman paused in his explanation to see if I were getting it. "Just like sunglasses block out some of the light but not all of it, these clouds blocked out the light from some stars."

"But I could see a few stars."

Herman laughed that knowing laugh again, then explained, "Some stars are far off . . . so they are dim because their light has to come millions of light-years through space. That means the stars that are closest to Earth shine the brightest." Herman continued. "Also, some stars are much bigger . . . so they shine more brightly." Herman and I walked to the door of the school. But I was not finished with my questions.

"Why are some stars bigger than others? . . . And why are some stars closer than others?"

"Well . . ." Herman stroked his chin. "The big ones are big because God wanted them big, and those far away are where God put them." He stopped and looked down at me.

"Let me ask you a question." Herman looked over the edge of his glasses. "Why do you put basketball pictures in one place in your room and astronomy pictures in another?"

"Just because." I couldn't finish my answer because I didn't have a reason.

"Well, God puts stars where He wants 'em." Herman paused. "Just because . . . and He doesn't need a reason."

"How many stars are up there?" I asked.

"Hmmm . . ." Herman breathed hard as he answered. "I knew a fella named Abraham a few thousand years ago who thought there were about 3,000 stars up there."

"Why?"

"'Cause that's all Abraham could see with his naked eye." Then Herman acted like he knew something he shouldn't tell me, but he told me anyway. "I had some other friends who ground glass to make a telescope. When they made the first tele-scope, it was not as powerful as yours. They could count only about 10,000 stars."

"Wow!"

"They thought 10,000 stars were a lot, but they didn't have any idea how many were really up there."

"How many are there?" I repeated my question.

Herman didn't immediately answer me. He scratched his head, then spoke as if letting me in on a secret.

"When your mother attended this school, they called it P.S. 107. I was listening outside the door of her class one day. The teacher said there were over a million stars."

"Is that right?"

"Not even close." Herman laughed.

"Well, tell me . . . ," I insisted.

"That Hubble Telescope is a marvelous achievement of man. It's the most powerful telescope ever built. When I first saw that telescope, even I was impressed. They claimed to see over 400 billion stars with the Hubble Telescope."

"They claimed to see over 400 billion stars."

"Wow! . . . Double WOW!" I exclaimed. "Can they see all of them?"

"No." Herman shook his head knowingly. "No . . . not all of them." His smile told me he knew more.

"How many more stars are there?"

"Let's just say there are more than a trillion galaxies, and our galaxy has a billion stars in it. So it's probably more like a 100 billion trillion stars in God's universe."

"Why so many stars?"

Herman grinned at me and spoke slowly, his smile growing larger with each word, as though he were very pleased about the answer, "'Cause God likes stars."

CHAPTER 4

A Star Falls on Louisiana

I was still thinking about my conversation with Herman that night as I came in for dinner. So when the last story on the six o'clock news mentioned something about stars, it caught my attention. I ran into the kitchen to tell Mom what I'd heard. When I told her there was an emergency in Louisiana, she just laughed. But it wasn't a laughing matter to me. A meteor was falling toward southern Louisiana. I was afraid it would hit someone! Mom told me not to worry about it.

"It's just a star burning out," she said, then added, "Louisiana is a big place . . . besides, a falling star has never hit anyone."

That night, I directed my telescope out my window toward Louisiana, but I didn't see anything. No flaming meteor tail . . . no burning fire in the sky . . . nothing.

I wished Dad were still living with us. I was scared. I wanted to ask him about the meteor and hear him say it wouldn't hit anyone. When he and Mom were still together, we used to look at the sky and talk about the stars—just like I did with Herman.

I'll ask Herman, I thought. *He knows a lot about stars. He knows everything.*

The next day I had to look all over for Herman. He wasn't cleaning the boys' rest room. He wasn't pushing the dust mop in the hall. I finally found him sitting under the stairs.

"Will the Sun burn out?" I blurted out.

"Eventually." Herman laughed. "Why'd you ask?"

"Last night I looked through my telescope for the comet that's burning itself out over Louisiana," I explained, "but I didn't see it."

Then I explained that if a comet could burn out, so could stars, so could the Sun . . . then following my own kind of logic, I said, "If the Sun burns out, we'll enter an ice age."

Herman could see concern in my eyes. He knew I studied the stars. So he began his explanation at the beginning.

"A comet is not a star." He tried to take away my concern. "A comet is a gigantic piece of rock that's hurtling through space. Some comets are as big as a house. Some are as big as this state. Some are as big as Earth." Herman explained that some comets move in an orbit that comes near several galaxies.

"Halley's Comet comes within miles of Earth every seventy-six years." Herman circled his index finger widely around his other hand, which was made into a fist to resemble Earth.

"That burning light over Louisiana is not a comet. A comet follows a continuous orbit." Herman went on to explain that billions of oddly shaped asteroids or planetoids are whirling through space. When one touches Earth's atmosphere, it comes in so fast that the air is heated and its gases glow brightly. The streak of light that looks like it has a tail is called a meteor. Herman said most meteors burn up before hitting Earth.

"Like the one they saw over Louisiana," Herman stated matter-of-factly. "It never hit the ground."

"Whew!" I sighed with relief and walked to the window to gaze at the Sun. As I turned back, I said to Herman, "Will the light in the Sun go out?" But Herman was gone, and Mikey from my class was standing there.

"What?" Mikey asked. I was so surprised that I didn't answer him, so Mikey shrugged his shoulders and headed off to P.E. I wanted Mikey for a buddy, and we always talked at school, but we were never really friends. It was time for class now, so I left. Anyway, I had meant my question for Herman. I could hardly wait for the bell to ring so I could look for him. He was in the janitor's room.

"Why'd ya leave?" I innocently asked.

"I didn't see Mikey coming." That was a strange answer. Anyway, my favorite expert on stars picked up right where we left off.

"I never said the Sun wouldn't burn out," he explained. "I said comets don't burn, but stars burn . . . so they can burn out."

"Does that mean the Sun will stop shining?"

"Yes."

"When?"

"Eventually."

"How long before 'eventually' gets here?" I wondered out loud.

"Not in your lifetime," Herman replied.

"When?" I persisted in my question.

"The Sun is 5,000 degrees Fahrenheit at the surface, and 14 million degrees at its core." The janitor explained that was not an exact temperature, but it was close enough for me to get the picture.

"The last time I checked," Herman explained, "the Sun was cooling at such a slow rate every one hundred years that it was barely noticeable. It's cooling because the gases or the fuels that feed the fire in the sun are being burned up."

"So the Sun *will* burn up?" That made me nervous.

Herman explained that if nothing happens . . . and he repeated for emphasis, "If nothing happens in 100 trillion years, the fire in the stars will go out."

Then Herman said after the fire goes out, the star remnants float around for ten trillion, trillion, trillion years. Herman held up three fingers to emphasize three times a trillion.

"After that, the black holes suck up all the remnants in another 10,000 trillion, trillion, trillion, trillion, trillion, trillion, trillion years." Then Herman held up seven fingers to emphasize seven times a trillion.

"Then it's lights out." Herman grinned. "If the Lord doesn't come first."

"You mean everything will vanish?"

"Nothing goes on forever . . ." Herman paused. "Except God and people."

Herman tugged at the belt of his work trousers, then looked out the window into the sky as if looking for an answer. "God is eternal, which means He never began and He will never end." He explained that I had a spirit that was a reflection of God. It would never die.

"Does everyone have a spirit?"

"Yes."

"Everyone? . . . Including you?" I let the words trail off.

Herman didn't answer my question because it really wasn't a question. He didn't tell me if he had a spirit. Instead, he changed the subject.

"You want me to tell you what's gonna happen?"

"Yeah!"

*"God lives in heaven . . .
not in the sky where birds fly."*

"The Bible says God lives in heaven . . . not in the sky where birds fly . . . not in the place where we see celestial stars in their galaxies . . . but the home God lives in is called heaven."

"Where's that heaven?" I asked.

"Wherever God lives."

"Can I see it through my telescope?"

"No."

"Can it be seen through the Hubble Telescope?"

"No."

"Then how do you know it's there?"

"I've seen it," Herman drawled with a wide grin. "We can go there."

My eyes got big. Herman said we could go where God lives.

"The Bible tells us all about heaven," Herman explained, "and those who believe in Jesus can go there because He is the way to heaven."

Herman explained that in heaven there'll be no sun, neither moons nor stars (Revelation 21:23).

"No sun," I repeated Herman's words. "How can we see anything in heaven if there is no light?"

"God will be the light in heaven," Herman said.

CHAPTER 5

God Is Awesomely Big

As I walked down the hall after school, with my book bag thrown over my shoulder, I was in a happy mood. The bright sunlight glistening off last night's snow lifted my spirit. The tune I was whistling bounced off the empty halls, "I want to teach the world to sing . . ." Then I saw Herman coming toward me, dragging a large, plastic sack filled with wastepaper. I waved and yelled out the first thing that came to my mind:

"It's a big, bright, wonderful world today, isn't it?"

"If you only knew . . ." Herman stopped to pull a handkerchief from a rear pocket to wipe his hands. Then he looked out the window across the blinding snow toward the sun. "Do you know just how big this wonderful universe is?"

Pausing at the window, I squinted my eyes as I tried to look at the Sun.

"No, how big *is* the universe?" I asked. I knew I'd get an answer. Herman knew more interesting stuff than any teacher. He was probably the smartest person I had ever met.

"Ha . . . ha . . . ha . . ." Herman laughed.

"Do you really want to know how big this universe is?"

"Yeah."

"Close your eyes and face the Sun," Herman instructed.

"Okay." I could feel the warm sunlight on my face as I did what he told me.

"That warm ray just traveled 93 million miles from the Sun to Earth."

"How long did it take to do that?"

"Technically, light travels 700 million miles an hour," Herman said. "So it didn't take long, considering the best major-league pitcher can throw a baseball only a hundred miles an hour."

"That's awesome." I shook my head in amazement.

"That's only the beginning." Herman told me to look away from the Sun and open my eyes. He explained, "Our Sun and our solar system are not the only ones in this galaxy we call the Milky Way."

"Yeah . . . I've been reading about all the stars. There are a lot of suns in our Milky Way."

Herman said, "Our Milky Way is so large that it takes a light beam 100,000 light-years to travel from one end to the other."

Then Herman reminded me that light travels at the speed of 700 million miles an hour—much, much faster than a baseball at a hundred miles an hour. "Now let's go to the end of the Milky Way," Herman said.

"That's too far," I said, laughing. "I gotta be home for supper."

Herman smiled. "I don't mean traveling there in a spaceship. You couldn't do that now, but someday I'll show you how we *can* do it." Then he explained how we could go through space in our imaginations.

"Let's build stairs to the stars in our minds!" Herman challenged me.

"Yeah . . . that'd be cool." I waited for him to tell me how we could do it.

"Let's build the stairs out of paper," Herman said, coaxing me to dream.

"Paper stairs would fall down," I argued.

"Let's build stairs to the stars!"

"No, no," he said, "follow me into the stockroom." We cut through the secretary's empty office. Herman walked over to shelves packed with supplies and picked up a ream of paper in a blue wrapper. "These packages of paper will hold me," he explained. "Sometimes I stack several packages on the floor so I can reach the top shelf." He then stacked four packages on the floor and stepped on them. The four packages were about a foot tall.

"Pretend the thickness of one sheet of paper is the distance between Earth and the Sun." Herman held a piece of paper between his thumb and finger. He told me that a piece of paper is less than one-thousandth of an inch thick.

"Okay."

"We'd need stacks of paper stairs that are 22.5 feet high to reach the nearest star in the Milky Way." Herman explained we would need many more billions of sheets of paper to reach the next sun in the Milky Way.

"That's a long way," was all I could say.

"To reach from the bottom of our Milky Way to the top would take a stack of paper stairs that is 310 miles high."

"Wow! Our Milky Way is big." I was amazed by the universe.

"But let's travel through all the galaxies and through all the different universes," Herman said, then he asked me to imagine the tallest stack of paper I'd ever seen.

"To climb to the farthest star on the edge of the universe would take paper stairs 31 million miles high. Now remember," he said, "the thickness of every sheet of paper is the distance from Earth to the Sun."

"How'd the universe get so big?" I questioned.

"God," was the only thing Herman

said. Then he repeated what I had heard back home in Sunday school. "In the beginning God created the heaven and the earth" (Genesis 1:1 KJV).

"But I heard about the Big Bang," I told my friend, who was now replacing the packages of paper on the stockroom shelves. He didn't seem to hear so I repeated what I had said, "I heard that everything came from a Big Bang millions of years ago."

Herman may not have been standing in a classroom, but he was a wise teacher.

"If everything came from a Big Bang," Herman explained, "then there would still have to be something that caused that Big Bang." He laughed. "God spoke—and BANG!—there it was."

Herman told me how everything had to come from something, and everything comes from God. Only God is big enough to make a big universe. And only God is wise enough to put everything in place and make everything run according to His plans.

"Because God is big, He created a big universe."

"Awesome . . . ," I whispered in delight. "God is awesomely big!"

CHAPTER 6

Yellow Makes People Happy

A single yellow daisy growing in the window box in the school secretary's office caught my attention. I was fascinated with its corn yellow face that turned up to the sun. Its dark brown center reminded me of graham crackers. The halls were quiet and the other kids were gone. I was waiting in the secretary's office for my lost book bag. Someone had turned it in, and the secretary had gone into the principal's office to get it for me. I reached out to touch the perfect yellow petals of the daisy to see if they were real . . . or plastic.

"Daisy will get mad if you touch her." A voice halted me just as I was about to touch a petal. I jerked back my hand and turned around quickly. I had been caught.

"Don't be frightened." Herman smiled at me over the glasses on the tip of his nose. He continued. "Daisies are like dogs sleeping in the sun—they'll growl if you disturb them."

"I didn't mean anything," I quickly apologized. "Is it your flower?"

"No, the *Bellis chrysanthemum* belongs to the secretary." He bent at the waist, stooping over to get a closer look at the daisy.

"*Bellis chrysanthemum* is the botanist's name for this beautiful creation of God."

"Why'd they call it a daisy?"

"Someone probably said to it, 'Good morning, Daisy,' because the *Bellis chrysan-*

themum reminded him of a woman named Daisy who was bright . . . and sunny . . . and cheerful.

"Isn't that right, Daisy?" said Herman, talking to the flower. Then he grinned and nodded his head approvingly as if the daisy were talking back to him. "Uh-huh . . . Uh-huh."

"Can a daisy hear you?" I asked.

"It's alive," Herman answered. "God gave it life." Herman's kind blue eyes made me believe him as he spoke.

"Did God make this daisy?"

"He made the first one."

I stopped to think about the first daisy. Then I asked, "What happened to the first daisy?"

"It died," Herman said. "All plants eventually die."

I looked back at the bright daisy. Herman picked up a spoon in the flower box and scratched in the dirt around the daisy's roots. "She can breathe better if we loosen the dirt."

"How'd this daisy get here?" I asked.

"When God made the first daisy, He put a seed right in the middle of that graham cracker center." Herman pointed into the tiny deep brown cushion.

"That seed is alive with hundreds of little daisies that will bloom and grow." Next, Herman pointed to the dirt.

"If you plant a daisy seed in God's dirt, it'll grow into a daisy flower."

"How come dirt grows things?" I wondered out loud.

"God made the ground with life-giving nutrients," Herman explained. "There is enough life in the dirt in this flower box to grow beautiful flowers . . . or a juicy tomato."

"It's that simple?" I asked.

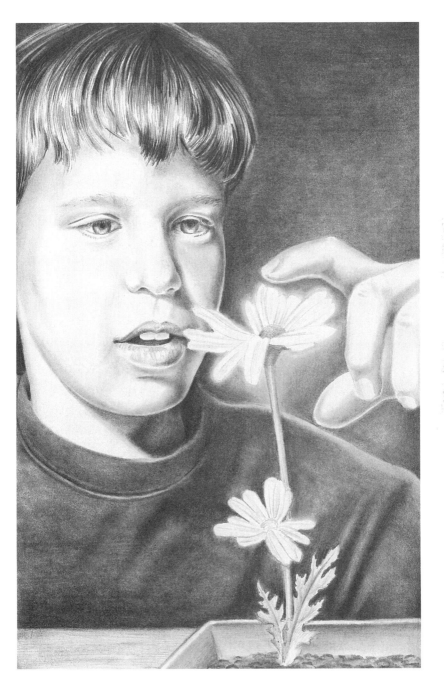

"When God made the first daisy, He put a seed right in the middle of that graham cracker center."

Herman smiled as though he knew more than he could say. He seemed to like all my questions. I really liked the way he explained things to me.

"Well," Herman said, chuckling, "to grow daisies, or even little boys for that matter, God put life in water and in the Sun, too." He pointed to the afternoon Sun. "Daisies get their life from the Sun."

"Wow!"

"God made everything," Herman slowly explained. "God made the Sun . . . God made the water . . . God made the dirt . . . and God made the daisy seed."

"Why'd He make the daisy yellow?" I asked.

This question seemed to stump Herman. He waited a few seconds, but not because he didn't know the answer. He really knew almost everything. Then smiling and speaking at the same time,

Herman said, "There's yellow in the Sun . . . and God put a tiny ray of sunlight in every petal."

I nodded my head in approval.

"There's yellow in the seed. And God spread it on the daisy, just like you take a knife and spread butter on toast," said Herman.

I smiled and nodded to let Herman know I understood.

Then he added, "God made the daisy yellow, because yellow makes people happy."

CHAPTER 7

The Universe Within

I had been looking everywhere for Herman. I had a question that just wouldn't go away, and I knew my new friend always had answers. I thought he might be in the stockroom, but Miss Stepak, the school secretary, wouldn't let me go in there. I asked her if Herman were there.

"Herman who?" she asked in a squeaky voice. As she leaned over her desk to look at me, a pencil fell out of her tall, curly hair, and her glasses slipped off the end of her nose and landed on her desk with a clinking sound. I jumped back in surprise—she was startled and dropped the telephone receiver she had been rest-ing between her ear and her shoulder. A stack of papers on the corner of her desk tipped over and fluttered to the ground around my feet.

"Herman . . . hmmm, Herman . . . uh, now where is my list . . . ," she mumbled as she gathered up the papers. Her phone began to ring again. I helped her pick up some of the papers and decided not to bother her anymore. I went to look for Herman myself.

Walking to the other end of the hall, I pushed open the door to the furnace room and yelled for Herman. No answer.

Where is he? I asked myself. Then I remembered the large oak tree on the other side of the soccer field. Once I had seen Herman eating his lunch there. So I headed in that direction.

"Looking for me?" Herman asked as I ran under the large overhanging branch that hid us from the school's view.

"This is a good place to talk," Herman explained. "Did you bring your lunch?"

I nodded and blurted out what was on my mind.

"Last night . . ." I puffed out my words between breaths. "Last night I heard something great on TV."

"What's that?"

"I heard a man say that the universe is as small as it is big. He said, 'Just like there are planets whirling around stars in every galaxy, that same thing happens in every small atom.'" After I'd finished blurting out what I remembered hearing, I asked, "Is that so?"

"Yup." Herman was leaning against the

trunk of the tree, his legs stretched over some roots growing on the ground. His "yup" answer was too simple. I wanted to know more.

"Have you ever seen inside an atom, Herman?"

"Well, my young learner . . ." Herman paused for effect like he always did. "Let me tell you about atoms. Everything in this universe is made up of atoms. They're the building blocks God used to make everything."

"Are carrots made of atoms?" I asked that question because Mom had put some carrot sticks in my lunch.

"Carrots and all vegetables are made of atoms," Herman answered as he looked inside my lunch bag. "So is the ground they grow in and the water that nourishes them."

"How about my hamster?" I pressed

Herman. "And how about Dad's dog, and how about me?"

"You're all made of atoms," Herman concluded. "Absolutely everything is made of atoms."

"Then how is an atom like a star?" I had to know.

"Atoms are made up of three things." Herman picked up three small stones. "Of course they're much smaller than these." He held up the three stones for me to see, then brushed a clean spot on the ground. He drew a circle in the dirt with a stick.

Holding up two stones, he said, "I'll call the first stone a proton and the second stone a neutron." Herman then placed the two stones side by side in the center of the circle and explained, "These two make up the center of the atom, like the Sun makes up the center of our universe."

Then Herman placed the third stone on the edge of the circle he had drawn in the dirt. "I'm gonna call this stone an electron." He pointed to the stone on the edge of the circle, explaining, "It revolves around the two stones in the center."

I nodded that I understood.

"That's your universe in every atom—electrons that circle around protons and neutrons," Herman said triumphantly as if he were finished with the lecture.

But I had another question.

I picked up a grain of sand between my thumb and forefinger and held it up to a shaft of sunlight shining through the branches. But before I could speak, Herman knew what I was going to ask.

"No, you can't see an atom." Herman laughed. He knew I was trying to see something really small.

"Atoms are made up of three things."

He told me, "*You* can't see atoms like *I've* seen them."

"How small are they?"

Herman reached over and took my ballpoint pen out of my pocket and pointed to the little ball on the end. "If an army of soldiers marched up to your pen, four at a time, and each one took only one atom from the ball, it would take 20,000 years for those soldiers to get every atom that's in the ink ball."

Reaching for my pen, I stared at the ink-covered ball, clicking it in and out several times.

"That's just the atom," Herman explained. "The protons and neutrons are much smaller."

"How much smaller?"

"Well . . . if you could place them end to end—which you can't do—but if you could, it'd take 2.5 million protons to make one inch." He stopped and held up his pointer finger.

"That's about as long as from your fingernail to your knuckle.

"Sit here," Herman instructed as he picked up a stick. "Keep your eye on these two stones—the ones we're calling protons and neutrons. I'm gonna show how much space there is in an atom. There's a lot more space in it than this little circle I drew in the dirt." Herman picked up the stone he called an electron and walked to the other side of the soccer field. He didn't stop until he was way on the other side of the schoolyard.

"I'm gonna draw a circle," he yelled back. Then with the stick he began to draw a line across the soccer field and continued across the playground. When he got to the sidewalk and road, the stick didn't make a mark, but he kept drawing the imaginary line until he came back to where he began. Then he yelled again, "I'm putting this electron down on the edge of the circle." He put the little stone down on the circle he just had drawn.

As Herman walked back to the tree where I was waiting, I understood what he was trying to tell me. Just like Earth was small in comparison to its gigantic orbit around the Sun, so there was a gigantic orbit in each atom. When Herman got back to the oak tree, he sat down to rest.

But I had other questions.

"If there's so much space between the electrons and the center of the atom," I said as I began to pound on the tree, "why doesn't my hand go through the tree, or at least sink into it?"

Herman didn't bang on the tree like I did. He took his index finger and tapped on the tree. "My finger doesn't go in this tree for the same reason you can't stick your finger in your bicycle spokes when the wheel is spinning fast."

I nodded because I thought I understood.

"The speed of the electrons," Herman said and tapped the tree again, "and the force of attraction make the tree hard." Herman grinned, and when he did that, I knew something was coming. "Another friend of mine named Einstein used to talk to me about the same thing."

Herman watched for my reaction, but I hadn't seen Einstein around school, so I didn't know who he was talking about. "Einstein was a great scientist who said everything is energy; in every atom is a world of power. Those electrons swirling around neutrons and protons are electric energy. That is the same energy that can cause an atom bomb explosion."

"Where did it all come from?"

"God made everything," Herman explained. "God is powerful. He packs some of His power in every atom."

As we sat under the oak tree on the other side of the soccer field, Herman explained to me that I was made out of atoms, just like the carrots I ate and my dad's dog that I played with on Sundays. Everything was made out of atoms.

Herman puckered up his lips to blow into his cupped hand. "When God made man, He breathed life into man, so that man was made in the image of God."

"What does that mean?"

"When you look in a mirror each morning," Herman explained, "you see yourself, but that's not yourself . . . that's only your reflection or image."

Herman thought for a minute, then explained, "When God looks at you, He looks at someone like Himself . . . He sees His reflection in you."

Herman and I talked a long time about people and how God made them. He told me how people are made of atoms, but because they are made in God's image, they are like God.

"God thinks, feels, and makes decisions just like we do; except that we're made like God, He's not made like us," Herman explained. "You are made in the image of God."

"You, too?" I asked Herman.

He didn't answer, he just smiled and grinned like he knew something he wouldn't tell me.

CHAPTER 8

A Guardian Angel

After dinner I went for a walk down by the lake. The lake looked really mysterious, all frosted with shiny ice. Lakes didn't freeze where our family used to live before the divorce. Dad had always promised to teach me to fish before the weather got too cold, but he had a lot of work to do and never did get around to it. After school that day, I had tried to call Mikey to see if he wanted to do something together, but he wasn't home. Everyone was busy. Even Mom.

"Don't go on the ice." Mom's words seemed to ring in my ears like a bell as I edged my right shoe out on the ice to see if it were solid.

I know I shouldn't be doing this, but I just want to see if it will hold one foot, I thought.

When the ice didn't crack, I put both feet on the ice, thinking, *It's shallow near the shore. If I fall through, I can just wade back out.*

"Easy does it," I gave myself a pep talk as I took one more step . . . then two steps . . . then three.

I decided to walk to the other side, just to say I'd done it. The ice cracked once, and I stopped in my tracks. I waited a few seconds then walked on, even though I was scared. I wasn't really worried; I'd passed my swimming test at school. I made it across the pond in a few more steps. That hadn't been so bad. The ice seemed really strong except for that one little cracking noise. I decided to walk back across, rather than go around.

CRACK!

Suddenly, the ice gave way with a sharp, piercing noise. Before I knew it, I was under the freezing water. I immediately began dog-paddling for the surface, but I bumped my head on the bottom side of the ice. I couldn't find the hole I'd fallen through!

I can't breathe, I thought, panicking. *Which way is the hole . . . ?*

Flinging my arms above my head in the cold water, all I could feel was hard ice. There was no opening into the air. I couldn't get out. I dog-paddled to the left, then came back. I was losing my breath. *Where's that hole?* I yelled in my mind. I was all alone.

I'm trapped and . . . I'll die!

The Moon shining on the ice turned the surface into a blue mist. *The Moon will be the last thing I'll ever see*, I thought, wishing I had told my mom where I was going. *No one would know to come looking for me here . . .*

Then a shadow blocked out the Moon. Someone was stomping on the ice with the heel of a boot.

CRACK! The ice splintered again.

"Grab my hand." It was Herman poking his calloused hand into the icy water. Pulling with all his might, he jerked me from the water right onto the ice.

"Let's get off this ice before it cracks again."

"Herman," was all I could gasp at first. Then, "Where'd you come from?"

"I was nearby, and I saw someone go under." He shrugged. "Good thing I was— or you'd be a goner!"

I can't breathe!

Taking off his blue and green jacket, Herman wrapped it around my already shivering shoulders. "Let's get you to your mom." He pushed me toward home. "Can you walk, or do you need help?"

"I'll make it . . ."

The front door was locked, so Herman banged on the glass. It rattled. He anxiously beat on the door again. "You'll catch pneumonia." Herman shook his head. "I'll go around back to get someone to come to the door."

As he disappeared around the house, Mom opened the front door. "Oh, Jacob! What happened?" she asked. But she must have known I'd fallen in the lake because she scolded as she rushed me upstairs, "I told you to stay off that ice."

I was cold—shivering cold and very tired. I must have fallen asleep for a long time.

A Guardian Angel

I awoke beneath warm covers. I could barely see the ceiling light between the two narrow cracks of my eyelids. I had stopped shivering, but my toes were still kind of numb. Mom was sitting by my bed with a cup of warm tea.

"How are you feeling?" she asked.

Suddenly I remembered everything. "Herman saved me!" I told her. "My friend Herman, who works at our school—he saw me fall in the lake. He pulled me out."

"I didn't see anyone with you . . ." Mom looked at me strangely. Then, worried about the friend who had saved me, she said, "I'll call the principal and see if I can find out if your friend made it home okay. Did you say his name is Herman? Is he a teacher?"

"No, he just takes care of things, cleans and stuff," I said.

"Well, I'm sure he's fine." Mom smiled.

"And we should thank him for being so brave." She gave me a hug and went to call about Herman.

Mom came back a bit later with a puzzled look on her face and said, "Jacob, they haven't hired a new janitor at your school since Mrs. Thompson retired at Thanksgiving. The principal doesn't know of anyone who works there named Herman." She looked at me in a worried way and put her hand on my forehead. "You feel a little feverish," she said and put the thermometer in my mouth.

It fell out when I said, "Mom, I'm telling the truth. Herman was there! He had just gone to try the back door when you came and found me out front."

"Okay, okay, I believe you." She put the thermometer back in my mouth and patted my cheek. "Now close—keep this under your tongue."

Just then the doorbell rang, and Mom went downstairs to answer it. Someone was talking to her as they came back up the stairway. "Well, it looks like someone was there, I saw two sets of footprints in the snow from the broken ice up to the front porch." It was Dad's face that appeared around the corner. "Dad!" I yelled, and the thermometer dropped onto my bedspread again. Mom grabbed it before it could roll off the bed and put it back under my tongue.

Then I heard another set of footsteps coming, and Mikey popped his head into the room. "Hey, Jacob, looks like you almost drowned! Your dad and I went down to the lake to see what happened. Wow, I'm glad you're okay."

"Mikey, you know Herman, the old guy who cleans up at the soccer field and the school," I said, glad to have someone to back me up. I knew Mikey must have seen Herman there sometime.

"That guy you told me about, the one who knows all about stars and stuff?" he asked. "Well, I've never really seen him myself—I've just heard about him from you."

Mom and Dad just looked at each other. Mom picked up the thermometer off the floor and looked at it closely. Dad looked over her shoulder. "Hmmm . . ."

"Whose coat is that?" Mikey said, spying Herman's big, blue and green jacket drying out on the back of my chair.

"All right! That proves it," I yelled. "That's Herman's jacket. He always wears that jacket."

My parents didn't seem convinced. As they went out of the room, I heard Mom saying, "It must have been a passing motorist . . ."

A Guardian Angel

"I believe you, Jacob," said Mikey, plopping down next to me. "Sounds like we have a real mystery on our hands, but we'll get to the bottom of this. Tomorrow at school we'll do a little detective work together. Now, tell me everything that happened . . ."

The next day Mikey and I went to the stockroom. There was no sign of Herman. I glanced out the front door of the school to check on the flag. It was already up.

The secretary had not seen the man I described around the school. *How could we check up on Herman?* Then I remembered all he told me about stars.

We went to the library to read in the encyclopedia about stars and comets and moons and suns. It was all there, just like Herman had told me. Even the information about atoms was the same.

"What about all the things you told me

Herman said about God?" Mikey asked. "My uncle is a pastor, and he knows a lot about the Bible. Let's ask him."

We stopped at Mikey's uncle's church after school. I told him what Herman had said about God creating everything and about heaven. He showed us places in the Bible where it told about creation. Stars, heaven, light—even flowers! It was all there just as Herman had told me. I liked what it said about God.

"You can come to Sunday school with me sometime if you want to hear more about the Bible," Mikey invited. I thought I'd like that, too. Mikey was a great guy, and he seemed just as happy as I was that we were doing something together outside of school.

That night I was lying on my bed looking at the stars and wondering about what could have become of Herman. It was a real mystery, just like Mikey had said. And we hadn't gotten to the bottom of it—yet.

My telescope was set up right by the window where I had left it a few days ago. Without adjusting anything, I looked into heaven and saw a star that I had never noticed before.

Where'd that star come from? I wondered.

Then I remembered that Herman once told me that stars were another name for angels, although he had also told me angels were not the stars themselves.

Could that be . . . ? The question shot through my mind.

I quickly looked again at the star. Sure enough, it was still in the same place where there had been nothing a couple of nights ago.

Could it be Herman trying to tell me something?

Then I thought I heard him laugh, just the way he always laughed when he answered one of my questions. I looked around, but no one was in the room.

I looked for the star again, but it was gone. It had just disappeared.

EPILOGUE

That Saturday I stayed over at Mikey's house and went to his uncle's church Sunday morning with his family. The man who taught his Sunday school class had a *really* interesting lesson waiting for us. Mikey and I nudged each other when he read a Bible verse that said this:

"Be not forgetful to entertain strangers: for thereby some have entertained angels unawares" (Hebrews 13:2 KJV).

Suddenly the mystery about Herman seemed to have an answer.

We asked the teacher about angels. He read us a verse from Matthew 18:10 that he said told about guardian angels who watch over people. When we asked about angels being like stars, he told us how the Christmas shepherds saw a bright light in the sky when the angels came to tell them about Jesus' birth and how the wise men followed a very unusual star to find Him.

"Angels are pretty mysterious creatures," he said, smiling. We agreed.

I had seen Herman when no one else had. I had never once thought he was an angel. Had I been entertaining an angel unawares?

Herman told me things about the stars that I could have found out from books—but it would have taken me a long time to read all of the things I learned from him. I enjoyed listening to Herman and hearing all the things he told me, just the way he said them. He used my love for the stars to tell me about the God who created them.

Herman told me that he felt he had been given an assignment by God. I thought he was just talking about his work cleaning up around the school. Now that I look back on the accident on the ice, I think Herman's "assignment" was to save me!

The next week, Dad was teaching me how to make fishing flies, and I asked him about Herman. He thought about it for a while as he was choosing which string to use to wrap tiny feathers around a hook.

Finally, Dad just smiled at me and said, "Herman must have been your guardian angel."

A girl at school told me and Mikey there are no such things as angels. But I know my angel named Herman was there when I needed him most.